THE CASE OF THE
WATERY GRAVE

Anne Schraff

SADDLEBACK PAGETURNERS · DETECTIVE ·

PAGETURNERS

DETECTIVE

The Case of the Bad Seed
The Case of the Cursed Chalet
The Case of the Dead Duck
The Case of the Wanted Man
The Case of the Watery Grave

SCIENCE FICTION
Bugged!
Escape From Earth
Flashback
Murray's Nightmare
Under Siege

SPY
A Deadly Game
An Eye for an Eye
I Spy, e-Spy
Scavenger Hunt
Tuesday Raven

ADVENTURE
A Horse Called
  Courage
Planet Doom
The Terrible Orchid Sky
Up Rattler Mountain
Who Has Seen the
  Beast?

MYSTERY
The Hunter
Once Upon a Crime
Whatever Happened
  to Megan Marie?
When Sleeping Dogs
  Awaken
Where's Dudley?

Development and Production: Laurel Associates, Inc.
Cover Illustrator: Black Eagle Productions

SADDLEBACK
EDUCATIONAL PUBLISHING
Three Watson
Irvine, CA 92618-2767
Website: www.sdlback.com

ISBN-13: 978-1-56254-390-7
ISBN-10 1-56254-390-3
eBook: 978-1-60291-248-9

Printed in the United States of America
10 09 08 07   9 8 7 6 5 4 3 2

CONTENTS

Chapter 1

The mysterious accident had been in all the papers. Bob Pasquale had been working for Drake Detective Agency for about a year then. Anson Ledyard, a millionaire computer businessman, had vanished. A week later his Lexus had been found submerged under 10 feet of water in a Florida swamp.

But the man's body was missing. Since the driver's side door was open, the police speculated that the millionaire must have been thrown from the car. And because the swamp was infested by crocodiles, Ledyard was presumed dead. But heavy rains had hit the area right after the accident. That made it entirely possible that Ledyard's body had been carried off into one of the many surrounding waterways.

And then, of course, there were the always hungry crocodiles.

The case file was sitting on Bob's desk. Tommy Drake, Bob's boss, was an ex-cop. A pair of bullets in his leg had forced early retirement. But the man still had detective work in his blood. Now Tommy stood before Bob and explained the situation.

"The insurance company wants an independent investigation of Ledyard's disappearance. There's a whole lot of insurance money at stake," Tommy said. "So, Bob, my man, we're going to have to do some unusual investigating—if you get my meaning."

"I don't think I do, Tommy," Bob said. Tommy Drake was around 40—a handsome, athletic man with a flair for gangster-style clothes and hot music. He didn't seem all that much removed from Bob's generation, although he was 16 years older than his assistant.

Tommy leaned forward, heavy gold chains clanking around the neck of his black turtleneck sweater. "Ledyard's wife is *your* age, Bob. So you're the one to get close to the lady. I've pulled some strings, and you'll start showing up at some of the parties the lady attends. It seems that she's quite a party animal. You're going to be listening for clues— trying to find out if she had something to do with her husband's watery demise."

"You figure maybe she put a hit on him?" Bob asked.

"Could be. The Lexus lost its brakes at a real bad time. Was it a coincidence that it happened at a curve in the road with nothing ahead but swamp and snapping reptiles?" Tommy said.

"Maybe—maybe not. What you're gonna be doing is priming your antennas to check the lady out. Is she grieving? Is she glad the old man was offed? Who knows—they might have been in on the accident together! Could be ol' Anson is off in some remote Shangri-la waiting for the big insurance settlement and their romantic reunion."

Tommy smiled. He almost always had a smile on his face. Bob smiled back. He really liked his boss. Everyone said that Tommy had been a great cop in his day. The man had gotten all kinds of commendations from the police department. Then a string of daylight jewelry store robberies had terrorized the city. Tommy ran the stakeout that netted the thieves. The crooks turned out to be coldblooded killers. They'd already murdered one jeweler, so the news stories had called Tommy Drake a hero.

Bob figured that shadowing Mrs. Ledyard wouldn't be too hard to take. Hanging out with the rich would be a nice change from his ordinary life. Right now he was taking college classes in the hopes of someday becoming a lawyer. His part-time job here at the detective agency was giving him good experience. The flexible hours were great, and the pay kept him in pizzas and blue jeans.

Usually, Bob would be investigating employee thefts from stores or trailing after unfaithful spouses. This would be his very first case involving a possible murder. It was pretty exciting.

Tommy gave Bob some upfront money so he could dress up for his new role. He was supposed to act the part of a rich but idle young man, newly arrived in the city. Bob got a big kick out of buying several pairs of expensive new slacks and shirts.

That night he met his girlfriend for dinner. "Don't let this go to your head," Jeri McNeil said as they ate their tacos.

Bob grinned. "Hey, it's just a job, Jeri," he said a little defensively.

"Yeah, right," Jeri went on, "driving a sportscar your boss rented for you and going to fancy parties every night and kissing up to what's-her-name—

Poopsie Ledyard. What a tough job it is to spend time with an incredible model whose glorious face and figure have been on at least 60 magazine covers!"

"The lady's name isn't *Poopsie*," Bob laughed. "It's Kelly—and we don't know what the deal is with her. For all we know, she might be a grieving widow who just wants a shoulder to cry on."

"Yeah, I'm sure she's just all broken up that her creaky old fiftyish husband died and left her with a billion dollars!" Jeri scoffed.

"Come on! You're sounding like a cynic, Jeri," Bob scolded her.

"Wouldn't *you* be jealous? I'm stuck in a dumb job coaching lazy students to use computers, and you're going off to glamorous parties to flirt with a super model," Jeri grumbled.

"Look Jeri—*usually* I'm following some slob down a dirty alley so we can get proof that he's cheating on his wife. Give me a break," Bob said.

"Yeah, but this time you hit pay dirt," Jeri said as she sipped some soda. "You're a cute guy, Bob—but do you really expect this babe to melt from your charms? You think she'll confess that she had her husband killed?"

"Of course not. I'm just looking for some clues to point us in the right direction," Bob said.

Jeri looked over at Bob as they pulled up in front of her apartment building. "Anson Ledyard was *megarich*, Bob. He must have given his wife a great life. And don't forget that *she* earned great money on her own. Why would she kill the guy for his insurance?" Jeri asked.

"I haven't got a clue. That's what I'm supposed to find out," Bob said as he kissed her goodnight.

Bob lived in a small apartment near the college. His parents owned a nice house in Butterfield, a small farming town about 600 miles away. Bob's dad had wanted his son to join him in the family business. But Bob couldn't see spending his life stuck in a little burg like Butterfield.

Before he went to bed, he glanced at a few magazines featuring Kelly's photos. There was no doubt about it— she *was* a totally gorgeous creature. He grinned wryly at her picture and said, "Hey, baby, why don't you give it up right now? Tell ol' Bob the truth—did you send your old man out to swim with the crocodiles?"

Chapter 2

The next evening Bob Pasquale was attending his first charity event. He had memorized his new identity carefully. Tonight he was the son of a rich old New England family that had made its fortune in shipping. He had moved down to Florida to go to school.

Bob made small talk with some of the other guests before he spotted Kelly Ledyard. Then he quickly moved into her path. "Hi! Great party—and all for a good cause, too," he said.

Kelly smiled. She was even prettier in real life than in her pictures. "Hi," she said. "Yes, it is a nice night for a party. It's so lovely out here on the patio."

"Oh, excuse me," Bob said, reaching out to shake her hand. "I'm Bob

Pasquale. I just moved here from Boston to go to school. I'm studying computer science—at my folks' insistence. But computers aren't really my thing. There's got to be something more interesting to do out there."

"Hello. I'm Kelly Bry—er—Ledyard," she said.

The disappearance of Anson Ledyard had been all over the newspapers and on television. It occurred to Bob that Kelly would think he was an idiot if he didn't know who she was. So he said, "Oh! I was really sorry to hear about your husband's accident. What a *terrible* thing! It must have been very hard on you."

"Yes, it was," Kelly said quietly. "But fortunately I've had some helpful grief counseling. Now I finally feel that I'm going to be all right."

"It's never easy," Bob said with a sympathetic smile.

"No, it's not," Kelly said. So far, Bob

thought she was very nice. And she seemed to like him. He hoped it wasn't just his imagination, but it appeared that she truly enjoyed his company. Usually, Bob had a good sense of how people were reacting to him.

"Have you been in the city long?" Kelly asked.

"No, just a few weeks. My parents wanted me to get some experience living on my own. I think they're afraid I'll never finish college and find a real career," Bob said.

"This is sure a beautiful place," Bob said. The patio was decorated with huge potted palms and exotic flowers for the party.

"My husband sponsored a lot of these charity events," Kelly said, "and this one was scheduled before—before his accident."

"Yeah. I remember reading about all the good stuff he did," Bob said.

"He was very generous," Kelly said.

There was a gazebo at the edge of the pool. The full moon reflected a milky glow on the water's surface, making a magical sight. Kelly stood in silence for a minute. Bob watched her closely, studying the unhappy look on her face. Was she thinking about the Lexus crashing through the guardrail that night? Was she feeling a wave of grief? Of regret? Of guilt? She looked miserable, that was certain.

"Are you okay?" Bob asked.

"Oh, yes," Kelly answered, as if snapping to attention. "Sorry, Bob—I guess my mind just wandered off for a minute. I'm fine."

"You want another drink?" Bob asked. Her glass was empty.

"Thanks. Another daiquiri, please. And bring me one of those caviar appetizers, will you? They aren't as good as the ones we get at Lorenzo's, but they'll have to do," Kelly said.

Bob quickly brought back the drink

and the appetizer. Then he and Kelly sat down on some wicker chairs by the pool.

"Are you still doing modeling?" Bob asked.

"My career is sort of on hold now," Kelly said. "I've gained a few pounds, and they want you to be totally gaunt. The trouble is, I could use the money. Anson's assets are all tied up for the moment. I don't understand all this legal stuff. Anson's adult kids, you know—"

"Oh, yeah," Bob said. While doing some research, he'd found out that Anson Ledyard had been married twice before he'd married Kelly. His three children from those marriages were grown now.

Bob studied Kelly's pretty face as she rambled on. After drinking for most of the evening, she'd became talkative. Bob felt guilty that he was happy about that. Alcohol really did loosen the tongue.

"Anson was a wonderful man—but he gambled, you know. He especially loved to gamble in Las Vegas, at the different casinos. I'm afraid he piled up some huge debts," Kelly said.

Had Anson gotten mixed up with mobsters? Was he murdered because of unpaid debts to the wrong people?

A shadow fell across the table as someone approached. When Bob looked up, a rather angry-looking young man was glaring down at them. "I've been looking all over for you, Kelly!" he said.

"Oh, hi, Jay. This is Bob Pasquale. He moved here recently from New England," Kelly said. "We've been talking about what a lovely night it is for this time of year. Bob, I'd like you to meet Jay Balfour."

Who was Jay, Bob wondered. A boyfriend already? If so, that was quick. Or maybe Jay Balfour had been around a while *before* old Anson went down to visit the crocodiles. . . .

Kelly held her empty glass toward Bob and gave him a little smile. "I need one more daiquiri," she said.

Jay grabbed the glass from her hand. "You've had enough!" he snapped.

"Oh, Jay, don't be like that," Kelly whined. "You know how hard it's been for me since—"

"I said you don't *need* anymore," Jay snapped. He'd become so angry that he'd forgotten to shake Bob's hand.

"Jay! You don't know what it's like. I can't even sleep nights!" Kelly cried, her voice rising to a high pitch.

"Just shut your stupid mouth!" Jay hissed. "You're *drunk*—that's what the problem is." Then he grabbed her wrist and pulled her to her feet. "Come on, let's get out of here!"

As Kelly tried to pull her arm free, Bob stood up. "Look, pal, don't be so rough on the lady," Bob said.

"No, *you* look, Bob whatever-your-name-is," Jay barked. "I don't know where you blew in from—but it's time for you to take a hike, okay?"

19

Bob was well-built, but Jay Balfour looked like he might have been a linebacker not so long ago. Bob figured that it wouldn't be a smart move to pick a fight with him. A brawl at the first party he'd been invited to would be the end of Bob's usefulness to the investigation.

So he watched silently as Jay led Kelly out to the parking area. Following at a discreet distance, Bob tried to hear as much of their conversation as he could.

"Get in the car!" Jay snarled.

"Jay, I'm so *scared*," Kelly moaned. "Every night it's the same. When I'm trying to go to sleep, I see his face looking up at me from under the water with those eyes, those piercing eyes. . . ."

"Just get in the car," Jay repeated.

"I can't stand it anymore, Jay!" Kelly cried. "It's like he's looking at me and saying *'How could you?'*" Then her thin shoulders started to shake with sobs.

# Chapter 3

Jay pushed Kelly into the car and slammed the door. Then they drove off, leaving Bob standing in the darkness, shaking with excitement.

He thought that Kelly Ledyard must be guilty of *something*. But was she guilty of arranging a hit on her husband—or just of not loving him? She seemed very comfortable talking to Jay Balfour. Bob took it for granted that Jay must know the whole story.

Bob's mind raced through the possibilities. Maybe Jay and Kelly were sweethearts. Maybe they'd conspired together to get rid of the rich husband.

Nah, that was too neat, Bob thought. But it sure wasn't *impossible*. Hey, it could just as easily be true! Sometimes the most obvious answer *is* the answer.

The next morning Bob reported what had happened to Tommy. As usual, his grinning boss leaned back in his swivel chair. His cowboy-booted feet were propped on his desk.

"It all went pretty well. I got real friendly with Kelly," Bob said.

"Good, good. So what's your gut feeling?" Tommy asked eagerly.

Bob told Tommy about Jay Balfour and the conversation he had overheard.

"Sounds like they have a thing going, right?" Tommy said. "That would be a good reason to off the old dude. But I'm not buying that. I don't care how many crocodiles live in that swamp. I think the police would've found *something*. Mark my words, Bob. I think Anson Ledyard is alive and kicking somewhere. And it's our job to prove that so we can get the insurance company off the hook." Tommy leaned forward then. "Try to make a date with her, Bob."

"I don't know. It might be hard to move in on Jay," Bob said uncertainly.

Tommy grinned, the gold filling in his front tooth gleaming. "Come on, you can do it, my man! I did some research on the girl. From what I've been told she's a pushover for handsome young guys like you."

As Bob walked to his rented silver BMW, he thought about how easy it would be to get used to this good life. Too bad it was only a temporary gig. Sighing, he punched in Kelly's phone number on his cell phone. Tommy had provided him with the number.

Bob got her voice recording: *Hi, this is Kelly. I'm not home just now. But please leave your name and number at the tone—and have a nice day.*

Bob said that he really wanted to see her and left his home phone number.

Over dinner that evening, Bob told Jeri about his day. He had learned his lesson. "Like that babe is going to call *me* back!" he laughed. "The only reason she was nice to me at the party was that she was smashed." Jeri seemed pleased with his comment.

But when Bob got home, there was a message on his phone.

"Hi, Bob, it's Kelly. Get back to me," her message said.

Bob rang her up immediately.

"Kelly," he said, "thanks for calling back. I've been thinking about you. I'd love to get together over breakfast. How about tomorrow morning?"

"Well—okay. There's a little coffee house off Calistoga. Have you ever noticed it? It's called Pierre's Brewhouse. Do you know where it is?" Kelly asked.

"Sure do, Kelly. See you around nine?" Bob said.

"That's good," Kelly said.

"You know what, Kelly? I'm worried about you. I think you need a friend. You've been through a real rough time," Bob said. He felt like a creep to be worming himself into her life like this, but that was what he was paid to do.

"Oh, you're so sweet," Kelly said.

The heartfelt gratitude in her voice made Bob feel even worse.

On the way to the restaurant the next morning, Bob worked out his strategy. He knew he had to invent a convincing story about himself. How could he make his presence in Kelly's life seem more believable? Otherwise, she was bound to wonder why he was around so much.

Bob spotted Kelly in a corner booth. She looked less glamorous than she had last night—but somehow she was even *more* lovely! Her long hair was pulled back in a simple ponytail, and she wore a bulky sweatshirt and jeans. Bob slid in next to her. "Kelly, right off I've got to tell you who I really am," he said.

Kelly smiled. "Good. I thought the story of the rich-but-aimless college student from New England sounded just a little bit fishy," she said.

Bob was well-prepared. To get some background on the case, he had studied Anson Ledyard's life. He'd discovered that Ledyard had grown up as an orphan in Texas. The man had made his money by his own grit and hard work. One of his favorite charities was the little ranch school in west Texas that had given him a home when he needed one. He was always raising money for the place. Every year Ledyard spent some time in old shirts and jeans mingling with the current residents of the school.

"Kelly, I *knew* your husband," Bob said with a shy smile. "I was one of the kids at Longhorn Ranch. I played ball with him, and I always thought it was pretty cool that a rich guy like that would care about us kids. So when I heard about his accident, I wanted to help his widow. You know—as my little way of repaying his kindness."

For a minute Bob feared that his nose was growing longer. That was something that was supposed to happen to liars.

Kelly blinked. "Oh, my goodness!" she cried out in surprise.

"When I heard about that accident, it was kind of like losing a foster father. And, I don't know—I just sort of felt I owed it to the guy to see if his wife needed any help. After all, you don't have a husband to protect you anymore, Kelly, and so—" Bob said.

"Wow, that's really touching," Kelly cried out. Her eyes brimmed with tears as she grasped her coffee cup with trembling hands. "I mean, how lovely *is* that!"

Bob gulped. He felt right at home with all those crocodiles slithering through the mud. Now he felt like one of their relatives—a snake.

Kelly was silent for a few moments, and then she said, "You know, my husband was a complex man. He was comfortable wearing dirty jeans and raggedy shirts, but then he'd insist on caviar from Lorenzo's every week! He was a hard man to understand. So charming and good-hearted one minute, and then—that explosive temper!"

"Your boyfriend, Jay, he seems to have a temper, too," Bob said.

Kelly looked startled. Then she laughed. "Oh, Jay's not my boyfriend," she said in an amused voice.

"I thought he was. Last night at the party he seemed real bossy," Bob said. "Like he had every right in the world to tell you what to do."

"Jay is Anson's son," Kelly said. "His oldest son."

"I see," Bob said. "Well, I suppose it's a good thing he's around to look after you. It's nice that you and your husband's kids get along. That's not always the way things work out."

As Kelly took another gulp of coffee, Bob noticed the dark circles under her eyes. She looked distraught.

"You've got it all wrong, Bob. Jay

hates me. He despises me," she said. "All three of Anson's children do. But especially Jay. Balfour is his mother's last name. He had his name changed because he hated his father so much.

"You know, Bob, the night the accident happened, *I* was supposed to be in the car with Anson. When the Lexus went into the swamp, we would have *both* died in those murky waters! Somebody on TV said that swamp is loaded with crocodiles . . . Except for a last-minute change of plans, I could have been eaten by them, too!"

Chapter 4

"But if he hates you, Kelly, why do you let him hang around?" Bob asked. "I wouldn't get in a car with a guy who hated me that much. Why did you go off with him last night?"

"I've always tried to be nice to Anson's children. Believe me, I've really *tried*. And now the lawyers are telling me that the children could tie the estate up *forever* if they wanted to. And the truth is that I'm really kinda strapped for money, Bob. If I play hard ball with Jay, he could make my life really miserable," Kelly said. "So I let him, you know—give me advice and stuff."

"Kelly, you said you were supposed to be in that car. What did you mean? Do you think by any chance that it *wasn't* an accident? Could somebody have wanted you and your husband out of the way?" Bob asked.

Kelly cradled the coffee cup in her trembling hands. "I'm not really sure about anything anymore. I guess I'm pretty naive. I was just a girl when I met Anson at a beauty pageant, you know. He swept me off my feet."

Her face looked sad. "I'm not very clever. Like the money I made as a model. I don't know where most of it is. My agent made some bad investments, I think. And Anson—he gambled and got mixed up in the stock market. I was never very sure what was going on."

Bob looked at the young woman's unhappy face and felt genuine sympathy for her. She was clearly out of her depth. No doubt she was just a pretty young girl who had been thrust into a world of power and wealth, maybe even crime.

"I just want you to be safe," Bob said. He was sincere, at least, in that. For a minute he forgot that he was Tommy Drake's man—whose only reason for being here was to save the insurance company a bundle.

"That's so sweet of you," Kelly said. "I really appreciate it, Bob."

"You know, Kelly, they never found your husband's body. Do you feel *sure* that he's actually dead?" Bob asked.

Kelly's eyes swelled with tears. "How can you ask such a thing, Bob! *Of course* he's dead! If he were still alive, wouldn't he be here with me? Where would he be?" she cried out emotionally.

"I don't know, Kelly. There might be a very good reason. Sometimes people are injured in accidents, and they forget who they are. You know, they have amnesia," Bob said. He didn't want to voice what he was *really* thinking—that Anson Ledyard may have had a financial motive to disappear. Maybe he took several of his millions and went off to Brazil, leaving his young wife behind to battle the insurance company and his tangled financial affairs.

"But that's *impossible*. Somebody would have seen him by now!" Kelly said. "Oh, no, Bob, he's dead, all right. There's no doubt that he's dead." She started to cry then, her whole body shaking. "Those horrid crocodiles . . . they don't leave much behind!"

 # Chapter 5

After a few minutes, Kelly stopped crying and dried her eyes.

"I just want you to be careful," Bob told Kelly, grasping her hand.

"I will," she promised. "You're such a sweetheart. You're the only man who has been genuinely concerned about me in ages. Girls always envy models, you know—but they shouldn't. Every man I've ever known just wanted me for his own reasons. It won't surprise you to know that Anson called me his 'trophy wife.' He liked to show me off. Then when I gained a few pounds and my modeling career started to go sour, he—he taunted me. He said, 'Well, fatso, now you better be nice to me, because I'm where your bread is buttered.'"

She was silent for a few moments, looking down at the tabletop. Then she burst out, "Oh, Bob—I shouldn't even tell you this, but we had a terrible fight the morning he drove off in his Lexus. I told him I hated him—and—and I told him I hoped he had a wreck and was killed! He just laughed at me—and—and that's the last I ever saw of him."

"But you didn't really *mean* what you were saying, Kelly," Bob said.

"No, I didn't. But I feel so bad that those were my *last* words to him," Kelly said in a shaky voice.

Bob wondered if he was getting close to something important. She had just admitted that they had not had a happy marriage. Maybe in another few days she'd admit even more.

"Let's go to lunch tomorrow, Kelly," Bob suggested. "I know a marvelous little Italian restaurant."

Kelly brightened. "I'd like that. Oh, I would *so* like that. I'm awfully glad we met, Bob. You are so special. Most guys just hear the name Kelly Bryn and all they can think of is the swimsuit issue of that sports magazine. Then they drool like dogs—but they don't care about the *real* me. They don't even want to know me as a real person. To them I'm just some kind of fantasy."

Bob felt rotten again as he walked to his BMW. Here he was, pretending to be the friend of a poor little widow. And the truth was that he was playing on her vulnerability, hoping that she might betray herself. Oh, he was some *friend*, all right. He was lying to gain her confidence—just so some multimillion-dollar insurance company didn't have to pay off a death claim!

"What a creep I've turned out to be," Bob berated himself. "I'll be the kind of lowdown lawyer everyone makes nasty jokes about. Greedy, unscrupulous—a skunk who'll do anything to make sure his side comes out on top."

When Bob reached the BMW, he was surprised to see that Jay Balfour was standing there waiting for him. An extra-extra large sweatshirt covered the huge muscles of his upper body. Bob could imagine him on the football field, easily scattering other big guys in all directions like so many toy figures.

"I need to talk to you, guy," the big man snarled at Bob.

Bob made his face look innocent and surprised. "Okay, what do you want to say?" he asked.

Jay invited himself into the car and sat next to Bob. "I don't know what your racket is, Pasquale—that's your name, right? It sounds like some kind of squash. If you get in my way, man, you're gonna *be* squashed!"

Bob shrugged as if he didn't know what Jay was talking about. "Look, I don't want any trouble," he said.

"What's your game, buddy? What do you want with Kelly?" Jay demanded.

THE CASE OF THE WATERY GRAVE

"Just to help her out. I used to be a kid at the Longhorn Ranch in Texas—that place Mr. Ledyard ran for orphan kids. He was nice to me, and I'm trying to return the favor by helping his wife out," Bob explained. Kelly had fallen for that story right away. Jay Balfour looked like he might not be so gullible.

"Come off it, Pasquale!" Jay sneered. "You're nothing but a little preppie jerk who wheedled his way into a party you weren't invited to. Then you spotted this gorgeous chick and decided to make time with her. The fact that she stands to become a rich widow sounded okay, too. You think you hit pay dirt. Maybe you read about this charity deal in the papers, and your little weasel brain went to working overtime. You probably figured you could parlay your pretty-boy good looks into a relationship with this dumb chick. You figured you'd be on easy street."

Balfour spoke in a rough, angry

voice. His big hammy hands were balled into fists that bounced on his knees like basketballs. Bob was almost frightened into admitting that the Longhorn Ranch story was a fake. He thought fast. Maybe he should admit that he *had* crashed the party and was blown away by Kelly's looks. Jay Balfour looked like he might believe that story more quickly than the "poor little orphan at the ranch" story.

But then Bob decided he'd better stick with the story he started out with.

"No way," Bob said. "You got me all wrong. A lot of kids at the Longhorn Ranch were off on the wrong track—like me. Mr. Ledyard, he had a bad start in life, too. He would tell us kids that he'd had plenty of brushes with the law. But then he straightened out and made a good life for himself. Most of us there were borderline delinquents. He really *did* help us find a new direction in life— and I'm grateful for that."

Jay Balfour looked even angrier.

"That's a lot of bunk! He never even gave his *own* kids the time of day! After he ditched my mother, we hardly ever saw him. Then once or twice a year he'd act like a big shot and come around to pass out gifts—like that meant anything!" he said bitterly.

But Bob had done his research well. He was sure about the ranch and the part that Mr. Ledyard had played in helping the kids. As Kelly had said, he was a complex man. "I don't know anything about *your* life, mister," Bob said, doggedly sticking to his story. "All I know is that he spent a lot of time showing us how to ride the horses and just talking to us about stuff. Is that so hard to understand? I figured I *owed* him. Looking after his widow just seemed like the right thing to do."

"She doesn't need looking after. She's nothing but a dirty little gold digger," Jay snarled. "That old man never treated his kids decently—and now that he's croaked, this money-grubbing little model is trying to get the money for herself. I wish that *she'd* been in the Lexus when it took that dive! That would have been a good ending for both of them: *croc food*."

Bob looked steadily at the huge man beside him. On the inside, he was shaking with fear, but he tried to hide it. He tried to remember why he was here—to get at the truth of Anson Ledyard's disappearance.

"Do you think it was an accident when the Lexus took that dive?" Bob asked nervously.

A look of rage flared in Jay Balfour's eyes. For a minute Bob thought those ham hands might reach out and try to choke the life out of him.

Chapter 6

Jay Balfour's face twisted in disgust. "The old fool always flattered himself that he was a mechanic. He fixed his own cars. I figure he must have screwed up the Lexus somehow," Jay snapped.

"Well, I feel sorry for Kelly," Bob said. "She seems like an innocent kid alone in a big world she doesn't understand. I can't see any harm in just giving her a little moral support."

"She's a moron and a lush," Balfour said bitterly. "She doesn't need some jerk like you hanging around. It's time for you to get lost, Pasquale. *I'm* seeing that she doesn't get into any more trouble than she has to—and that's enough. Do you hear me? Take a hike, man. Is that plain enough for you?"

"I don't think so," Bob said. He gave the man a hard look and thought about his gun. As a private investigator, Bob had the legal right to pack a gun, of course. So far in his career he'd never even come close to needing it. He sure didn't want to use it to persuade an angry man to get out of his car!

Bob's hand inched a little closer to the shoulder holster under his coat. Just the *thought* of using a lethal weapon on another human being sent chills up his spine. But he had taken the advanced pistol course at the police range. If he had to, he knew how to use the weapon. He hoped he wouldn't have to—but he knew he *could* shoot Jay Balfour if it meant saving his own life.

"Look," Bob said in a calm voice. "Kelly lost a husband, and we don't know if it was an accident or murder. She told me she was supposed to be in that car when it went into the swamp. They made a last-minute change of plans. Think about it. If somebody *did* tamper with the car, Kelly was supposed to die, too. It doesn't seem that the girl has that many friends. I think she needs at least one good one—so I plan to stick around."

Bob grasped the gun under his coat. If the need arose, he could have it out in a split second.

"Think about it for a minute," Bob went on. "Maybe whoever killed Anson Ledyard—if he's dead—will try to finish off the job by trying to kill Kelly."

"What do you mean—*if* he's dead," Balfour seized on those words, his eyes turning almost savage.

"Well—no body was ever found. No remains at all. Until something of him is found, we aren't going to know for sure," Bob said.

"They said the crocodiles got him," Balfour cried. "Everybody knows that crocs are thick in that part of the swamp. When they get fresh meat there's no stopping them. It's a feeding frenzy. There wouldn't be anything left after they were through with him. Nothing."

Bob was shocked at how anxious this man was for his own father to be dead—to be eaten by crocodiles! Bob shuddered to think of how much resentment and hatred had built up over the years. Every last remnant of love had been destroyed. Jay Balfour actually seemed to be *relishing* the thought of his father dying in such an awful way! "You really hated your father, didn't you, Jay?" Bob said. "I don't think I ever met a guy who felt that way about his own dad."

Balfour seemed startled by the comment. He hadn't expected it. But then he sneered. "What was to like about the guy? He ditched my mother when I was eight. He tried every scheme in the books to keep from paying child support. He'd rather spend ten thousand dollars for lawyers to stall the payments than to give us even one thousand. He kept my mother in the courts for half her life, scratching for a few dollars. Sure, I hated the guy. My mother died still battling him for what was due her."

Bob shook his head. "Well, that was too bad," he said. "I'm sorry to hear it."

Jay's angry face now hardened in determination. "Now, believe me, I'm getting my share of the old devil's money. He never wanted me and my brothers to have a penny—but we're getting it now. It's time to cash in," Balfour said.

"You planning to fight Kelly for the money?" Bob asked, trying to make his comment sound off-handed.

"Listen, punk," Balfour said in a nasty voice. "*You* don't own a piece of this action. You're an outsider, okay? You got no business being within ten miles of Kelly. Unless you don't like the shape of your nose, you better clear out. Or I'll rearrange it for you."

"I think you'd better get out of this

car right now, big guy," Bob said.

"No little punk tells me what to do,"
Balfour snapped. He looked like he was
ready to take Bob apart.

Bob's hand slid under his jacket and
came out with the gun. "Get out—*now!*"
he said in a low voice.

Balfour's eyes narrowed. "You're
probably a little scumbag from the old
man's gambling connections, aren't you?
You're some kind of criminal," he said.

"Maybe *you're* the criminal," Bob shot
back. "Maybe you'd like for Kelly to end
up the same way your father did," Bob
went on, keeping his voice calm. "That
way there would be no argument about
the money. You'd have it all."

Jay Balfour looked like he wanted to
turn Bob's face into hamburger. For a
few seconds it seemed that even the gun
wouldn't stop him. The hair stood up on
the back of Bob's neck. "You heard me—
get out of this car now, man," Bob said,
forcing his voice to sound tough.

Jay Balfour had never expected the soft-spoken little preppie to be armed. Until now he'd seen Bob Pasquale only as a fortune-hunting wimp, chasing after a supermodel with money. A craven little jerk. He never expected the gun or the sudden steel in Bob's voice.

Balfour opened the door and got out. But before he walked away, he said, "You stay away from Kelly. I mean it. Mind your own business, Pasquale. I don't know just exactly what your game is. But if you're working for somebody the old man owed money to, tell your boss to lick his wounds and go ask the crocodiles for the money. I'm warning you—if you're after Kelly for her money, you'd better go find another rich chick."

Bob drove off, shoving his gun back in his shoulder holster with a deep sigh of relief. He'd never wanted to fire the gun. It made him sick to his stomach to imagine what *could* have happened. This detective work was okay as long as he was dealing with deadbeat husbands and penny ante thieves in department stores. But *murder*? No way. This was all getting too heavy for him.

Bob sped down the street, completely bewildered by all that had happened. He had come to this case figuring that Kelly—and maybe Jay—planned to kill Anson Ledyard and divvy up the insurance money. Now he believed that Kelly was innocent. In fact, he was really worried about her. It seemed clear that she didn't realize what she was dealing with. Jay Balfour wanted that money, and he wanted it *all*. He wouldn't stop at anything to get it.

That's what Bob thought, anyway. He was truly afraid that Jay Balfour had enough hatred in him to go far beyond simple greed. Now it seemed likely that he had tampered with Anson Ledyard's Lexus, hoping to kill the father he hated and the stepmother he despised.

But, from Jay's standpoint, two

unfortunate things had happened. By sheer chance, the stepmother had survived. And the crocodiles apparently had eaten every shred of proof that Anson Ledyard was dead. The insurance settlement—the big payoff—had thus become horribly complicated.

Chapter 7

That afternoon Tommy Drake sat in his office drinking his usual herbal tea. As usual, he sat tipped back in his chair with his feet propped on his desk. "What do you know, Bobby, my man?" he asked between sips of the hot brew.

"Jay Balfour, one of Anson Ledyard's sons, is looking like a good suspect. He's a big dude—a former football player. And he's not only *big*, but he's as mean as a cornered rattlesnake! The guy's made it quite clear that I shouldn't hang out with Kelly anymore. He seems absolutely determined to get his hands on his father's money. I think he means to try to cheat Kelly out of her share.

"It seems that Anson Ledyard wasn't very generous with his ex-wives and kids. A lot of rage has built up in Balfour. I can't say for sure, Tommy, but I'm beginning to think that Jay Balfour might have messed up the brakes on that Lexus. I wouldn't be surprised if *he's* the one who sent it into the swamp," Bob said.

Tommy frowned. "Uh-oh, I don't like the way this conversation is going, my man," he said, taking another sip of herbal tea. "Are you leaning toward thinking the man is dead? That doesn't sound real good for our client."

"Yeah, I think he's dead, Tommy," Bob said flatly.

"Not good. What are you hearing from the widow? Does *she* think her dearly beloved is gone from this earth?" Tommy squeezed a few drops from a lemon wedge into his tea.

"Yeah, she's pretty sure of it. She told me that she and Anson had a fight before he took off that day. Otherwise, she would have been with him in the car when it went into the swamp. Kelly seems sad about her husband's death. She's even feeling guilty because their final moments together were angry. Yeah, I admit it—I'm starting to feel really sorry for that girl," Bob said.

"No, no, *no*, Bobby! No falling in love with somebody you're investigating! Scratch that impulse right now. I got a feeling deep in my bones that the crocs *didn't* feast on that fellow. I still think he's hiding out somewhere," Tommy said with a small smile. "And I figure the little widow knows all about it. I hate to burst your bubble—but I think she's playing you for a fool, Bobby."

"That's wishful thinking, Tommy," Bob said. "You don't *want* the insurance company to have to pay. But tell me— where would Anson Ledyard be? If the whole thing was a scheme to collect his own insurance, it would be crazy. Why would he cooperate by laying low? He's a smart man. He's got to know that leaving no trace of a body would really complicate things."

Tommy grinned, showing his perfect white teeth and the single gold filling. His tiny hairline mustache twitched on his upper lip. "Maybe the little lady is a very good actress. That's how she gained your sympathy. After all, she's a model. Models have to act. You'd better believe that women can be really devious, Bob. Stick with her, my man. Make sure she gets so comfortable with you that she lets down her guard."

"I plan to. We're going out to lunch tomorrow," Bob said.

"Excellent. My research confirms what you've already told me. The girl drinks a lot. So encourage her to enjoy the spirits at lunch—get her a jumbo margarita," Tommy said. His eyes twinkled. "You know the old saying— *When the spirits flow, the secrets go.*" Tommy leaned back and laughed heartily at his own corny poetry.

When Bob walked out of his boss's office, he was feeling like a creep again. He was *using* Kelly—pretending to be her friend for his own purposes. Poor Kelly—used by everybody, including him. Bob was treating her like nothing more than a means to an end. And all the time, deep in his heart, he was beginning to really care for her.

Bob decided that he'd at least do something special for Kelly. He'd bring her caviar from that place she said she liked so much—Lorenzo's. Everyone said they sold the finest caviar in the city. It was costly, delectable, the best.

Lorenzo's was in a fashionable part of town. All the shops here catered to the wealthy people who lived in the palatial homes high up in the hills. You could walk these streets most any time and see some famous faces from television or the movies.

Bob's mind vaulted back to his own little hometown—or hick town, he should say—Butterfield. Here Bob was, the son of a Butterfield asparagus farmer, mingling with the rich and the famous. What was he doing here with all of these beautiful people, buying their fancy caviar from Lorenzo's?

Bob walked into the small gourmet grocery store and waited at the counter. A middle-aged man, probably a Russian, waited on the customer ahead of him. Bob didn't know a thing about caviar, but he thought it had something to do with Russians. He looked around and saw that the store sold all kinds of rare and exotic delicacies. A sign on the wall said that home deliveries were available for customers who didn't have time to come in for their treats.

"I'd like some caviar," Bob said.

The clerk sniffed as if he'd already detected that Bob wasn't one of his usual high-class customers. Clearly, he looked like a man who did not know his caviar. "What kind, sir?"

"Uh, I don't know much about caviar, but you used to have a real good customer. He bought caviar here every week. Mr. Anson Ledyard. I'd like the kind he bought," Bob said.

"Ah yes, yes," the man said, turning to the Asian boy behind him. "The blue containers. Royal Sturgeon. The kind you've been sending to Mrs. Ledyard."

Bob was disappointed that Kelly had been getting the caviar. His gift wouldn't be such a treat now. But still, he hoped she would see it as a warm gesture. Surely Kelly would appreciate the fact that he had listened to her and remembered what she liked. Hadn't she told him once that you can never get enough good caviar?

# Chapter 8

The next day Bob arrived at Kelly's apartment a little early to take her to lunch. He carried the package of Royal Sturgeon under his arm. When Kelly let him in, he put the package down and said, "I heard you say that you like this stuff a lot. I got you some so you wouldn't run out."

"What is it?" Kelly asked, peering into the bag. "Ohhh! Royal Sturgeon! Oh, Bob, how sweet of you! I haven't had any of this for such a long time. Ever since Anson—" her voice trailed off.

Bob felt a pang of disappointment. So, he thought, she *was* a liar. He'd just been told that the store had been sending it to her regularly.

Bob stood in the middle of Kelly's

kitchen and looked around. She no longer lived in the mansion she and her husband had occupied. She had rented this elegant townhouse soon after the incident. She must be paying a fortune for it, Bob thought—but there were small telltale signs that she was in financial difficulty. When she went to get her sweater, Bob noticed a pile of past due bills lying on the counter. Credit card balances that had not been paid. Department store accounts with past due balances.

As they drove off in Bob's BMW, Kelly talked about her modeling career, her high school days, even her childhood. "You know, Bob, the last time I was happy was when I was sixteen. I got my first modeling job then—and I don't think I've ever been as happy since. I just wish that I'd never entered that teen magazine contest and become a model. I wish I'd just met a plain, ordinary guy—someone like you—and gotten married and had a normal life."

Bob looked at her and smiled. He couldn't help feeling sorry for her. He wondered if he really was falling in love with her. But then he thought about Jeri. Jeri was a pretty girl, but not truly *beautiful* like Kelly. On the other hand, Jeri was so easy and comfortable to be with. Bob had often thought he might make a life with Jeri. But somehow it was hard to imagine spending a whole lifetime with Kelly.

"Do you ever think that your husband could still be alive?" Bob asked her as they neared the Italian restaurant.

"Of course not," she said.

"Do you ever hope against hope that he'll turn up?" Bob asked.

"No," Kelly said. "I'm sorry about what happened. But I—uh—wouldn't really want him back." Kelly turned her head sharply and looked at Bob. "I bet you're shocked at that. I know it sounds really cold, but I can't help it."

They walked into the Italian restaurant and found a secluded booth. Kelly ordered a drink right away, and Bob didn't try to stop her. There was a conflict inside him—between Bob, the friend who didn't want to see Kelly get drunk, and Bob, Tommy's main man, who had a job to do. After a moment's struggle, Tommy's main man won out.

"Anson was such a card," Kelly said, twirling her long-stemmed cocktail glass playfully. Bob could see that the liquor was already making her giddy. "He loved to play these goofy jokes. He knew I was afraid of snakes, so one day he hid these realistic-looking fake snakes in my bed. But he went farther than that. He rubbed them with oil and kept them in the refrigerator so they'd be cold and slimy. Then, when I was in bed—very groggy, just falling asleep—he dumped the wet, cold fake snakes right on top of me. They wriggled and slipped around just like real snakes! I just screamed and screamed. And Anson laughed so hard. He even took a video of how silly I was acting. Sometimes he showed it to his friends."

"That sounds a little sadistic to me," Bob said.

"Oh, he had this crazy sense of humor," Kelly said. "He told me how he used to needle his other wives too. Not so much with Jay's mother. He left her with the three kids and got his jollies by squeezing them financially. But the second wife—she had this nervous terror of being late for things. So Anson would always keep stalling when they were ready to go somewhere. He liked to keep her on tenterhooks until she was a wreck. The poor woman would get so antsy she could hardly stand it. Anson thought it was a riot."

"Your husband had a lot of different sides to him, didn't he?" Bob asked. "He funded that school and did a lot of charitable things. But he also liked to play these sadistic jokes on people."

"Oh, Anson never really *liked* women. He liked his male friends, and he liked doing things for orphan boys. But he told me once that he actually *hated* women. Did you ever see a picture of Anson, Bob?" Kelly asked.

"Yeah, I did," Bob said. The guy wasn't handsome. He had big ears and a long, pointed chin. He must have been ugly even when he was young. With age he had grown very heavy, and bags hung in folds under his eyes.

Kelly rambled on. "He said the girls in his high school had mocked him mercilessly. He could never get a date, he told me. So he worked very hard to get rich. After that he said he had *all kinds* of women friends! Then it didn't matter that he was short and squat and homely. The women were eating out of his hand because he was rich." Kelly sighed and said, "I don't think he ever forgave womankind for rejecting him when he was a young guy."

"Yeah," Bob said, thinking about it. What would it be like to be really ugly and not be able to get a date? How would it feel to have the girls you were dying to hang out with make fun of you? No wonder the guy was bitter.

"Even though he's dead, I think he must be laughing at what happened," Kelly said. "You know—how his body was eaten up, and now we can't settle the will. It was just the way he would have planned it. Me struggling, Jay harassing me, and the two of us tearing at each other like scorpions in a bottle." There had been an amused but strained smile on Kelly's face as she prattled on. But then it faded and she shuddered.

"So, what are you saying?" Bob asked. "That he made a deal with the crocodiles to eat him up so you wouldn't get to enjoy the money?"

Kelly threw back her head and laughed. It wasn't a happy laugh. It was a hysterical, out-of-control laugh—the kind of donkey-like bray people make when they're almost drunk. "Of course it's crazy. Poor Anson didn't *want* to be eaten by the crocodiles. He loved life. I never met a man who loved life more. He had an amazing zest for living. Sometimes he seemed to live just to make other people unhappy—but still he would laugh and laugh. Even when I cried, oh, how he would laugh!"

"Kelly," Bob asked slowly, "how could you have married Anson Ledyard? Did you ever really love him?"

A strange look came over Kelly's face. She grabbed the drink on the table and drained it. Her lips trembled as she stared into space. Now she seemed to be beyond drunk. She actually seemed a little mad.

Chapter 9

Then Kelly laughed again. But this time it was a deep, guttural laugh that didn't sound hysterical at all.

"*Love* him? Oh, Bob! I didn't even *like* him!" she said, catching her breath.

"Really? Not even when you first met him?" Bob asked.

"Oh, he was charming, all right. And it was very exciting that he was so rich. He could buy me anything and take me anywhere. We had one of those whirlwind courtships you read about. We went to Japan and Paris and the South Sea Islands. We had a fabulous wedding in Las Vegas. Several celebrities came as his guests. The actress who won the Academy Award a couple of years ago . . . *she* came to my wedding! Just imagine. And Anson gave me a huge diamond. I felt like a queen. But then the honeymoon came to an end, and I woke up married to this nasty, ugly little gremlin—a mean little *monster*!" Kelly grabbed for another drink, but this time Bob gently put his hand on her wrist.

"Time to go home, Kelly," he said.

Kelly sobered up a little on the way back to her apartment. As Bob drove, she looked into a small mirror and touched up her makeup.

"Don't believe half of anything I say when I've had a martini," she said.

"Oh? And just what part of your story *shouldn't* I believe?" Bob asked.

"Oh, all that stuff about Anson. I *did* sorta love him, I guess. I liked it when we'd go into the casinos. He'd be so proud to show me around! When handsome young guys would stare at us, Anson liked to say, 'Look at what I got—eat your hearts out, guys.' I have to admit it made me feel good that he was so proud of me," Kelly said. "But it wasn't enough," she said sadly. "I was going to divorce him anyway. I had to."

Bob almost drove off the road.

"*Divorce* him? You were getting a divorce?" he gasped.

"Yes. That's what the fight was about. Our last fight. I didn't hate him or anything—but I just couldn't stand being married to him anymore. It crossed my mind that it would solve everything if he had a wreck and died. It would just make my life so much easier. But I didn't think it would actually happen," Kelly said.

"Kelly, do you—uh—think it might be possible that somebody *made* it happen?" Bob asked.

Kelly didn't answer the question. She looked out the car window and said, "I wish they'd find something of him. Then we could have a decent funeral—a memorial or something. I want there to be a monument for Anson. It should say something about that ranch in Texas. He'd like that."

"Come on, Kelly, tell me the truth. Did somebody kill Anson?" Bob asked.

Her face was serious when she turned and looked at him. "The cops said there was something wrong with the brakes. Beyond that, I don't know anything. I guess somebody *could* have messed with the car. When he hit that curve and the car wouldn't slow down, there must have been *something* wrong with his brakes," she said, her voice trailing away.

Bob's heart started racing. Was she about to confess? Was she fragile enough to do that? The cold, calculating part of him was eager for that to happen.

A tear slipped down Kelly's cheek. "Bob, you may be the first man I've ever known who really cared about *me* as a person. I guess you're the first guy I ever trusted. So if I tell you what really happened, can I count on you not to tell anyone else about it?"

"What happened, Kelly?" Bob asked, his heart pounding.

"I have this mechanic friend. He'd do anything for me because he thinks it's so great that a supermodel would be nice to him. I asked him if he could mess with Anson's brakes a little bit. You know—do some little thing so the Lexus wouldn't stop on the highway. I didn't tell Rex that I wanted to *kill* Anson—and I really didn't. I just wanted him to have an accident. But then I heard that Anson was driving real fast around that curve before the car went off into the swamp. I had no idea he'd be near the swamp— or the crocodiles—" Kelly put her face in her hands and wept.

"Kelly," Bob said softly, "is this the truth or another lie? You lied about getting the Royal Sturgeon. I know Lorenzo's has been delivering that brand of caviar to you right along."

Kelly's eyes widened. "*What?* No!

No, Bob, I swear that they haven't!"

Bob drove over to Lorenzo's. A crazy, wild idea was building in his brain. But he couldn't rest until he checked it out.

Leaving Kelly waiting in the BMW, Bob hurried into the store.

"I need some more Royal Sturgeon for Mrs. Ledyard," he said.

"Do we deliver it to the same place?" the Asian boy asked.

"No, I can take it with me. What is that address again?" Bob asked.

"Palmetto Grove Lane at Hibiscus," the boy said. "Do you want the whole order—the Royal Sturgeon, the blood sausage, and the rye—just like always?"

Bob took the package and headed out toward the country.

"Where are we going?" Kelly asked. "I've got such a headache. I always get a headache when I drink too much."

Bob kept on driving until he came to Palmetto Lane at Hibiscus. He saw a big old house sitting back behind an iron gate. It was half hidden by oaks swathed in long tendrils of Spanish moss.

Bob got out of the car and walked to the gate. He rang the bell and shouted, "Delivery from Lorenzo's!"

The front door of the house opened. A short, squat man came to the door. He had a long straggly beard and unkempt hair. He never looked out at the BMW or the woman in it, but he stared intently at Bob. "It's about time. You have my caviar?" he demanded.

"Yes, Mr. Ledyard," Bob said.

He glanced up, startled. Then he looked out toward the street and stared at the BMW. "Kelly!" he shouted. "Kelly, is that you?"

Kelly stumbled from the car, her face a mask of horror. "Anson? No—you're dead! The crocodiles ate you when you fell into the swamp—" Kelly screamed.

"Rex told me what you asked him to do, you little witch. So I thought I'd give you what you wanted. All I had to do was shove the Lexus into the swamp and then hide out. And it's really been a gas to watch you and my dear son twisting in the wind as you try to get your paws on my money!" Anson Ledyard sneered.

Kelly grew pale. She looked like she was about to faint. Bob could see that she was trying to mouth some words, but they wouldn't come out.

Anson Ledyard threw back his head and roared with laughter. Then he grabbed the caviar, blood sausage, and rye bread from Bob's arms and vanished inside the house with it.

Bob took Kelly home. He sent for the doctor and waited until he came before leaving her there. The girl was in bad shape. It looked like she was having a full-blown nervous breakdown.

Outside Kelly's apartment, Bob made a call on his cell phone. He could just picture the grin on Tommy Drake's face when he gave him the news.

"You had it nailed from the start, Tommy. I've got to hand it to you. Anson Ledyard *is* alive and well—and I found him," Bob said.

"Hip, hip, hooray, Bobby, my main man! I thank you, and the insurance company thanks you. Good work! You'll have a fat bonus to take to the bank tomorrow," Tommy shouted.

* * *

That night, Bob told Jeri McNeil the whole story from beginning to end. "Admit it," Jeri said to Bob, pausing over her hamburger. "You were falling in love with Kelly."

"Nah—not for a minute. That girl left me cold," Bob said.

As Jeri hugged him, Bob thought to himself that he was getting to be a very good liar.

COMPREHENSION QUESTIONS

RECALL

1. How did Jeri McNeil feel about Bob's new assignment?

2. Where did Bob claim to have met Anson Ledyard?

3. What special treat did Bob buy for Kelly?

WHO AND WHERE?

1. Where was Anson Ledyard's Lexus found?

2. Where did Bob Pasquale meet Kelly?

3. Who felt he deserved to inherit Anson Ledyard's money?

VOCABULARY

1. Bob was assigned to investigate Anson Ledyard's "demise." What does *demise* mean?

2. Kelly said that models had to be totally "gaunt." What does *gaunt* mean?

3. Anson Ledyard made a fortune through his own "grit" and hard work. What does *grit* mean?

IDENTIFYING CHARACTERS

1. Who scolded Kelly for drinking too much?

2. Who was Bob Pasquale's boss?

3. Which character was thought to have been eaten by crocodiles?